One for the Road

Melissa M. Buhl

&

Brian C. E. Buhl

Published by Water Dragon Publishing
waterdragonpublishing.com

ISBN 978-1-962538-28-2 (Trade Paperback)

FIRST EDITION

10 9 8 7 6 5 4 3 2 1

for Melissa, actually

Acknowledgments

This story came about when Melissa asked for a story. She had the idea, and I had the words. But the words didn't initially fall in the right order, and it wouldn't be the story it is today without Jennifer Brozek's help. I also owe a huge thanks to my critique group. Their support gives me courage.

One for the Road

"DO YOU KNOW WHY I pulled you over?"

Tina wobbled on her broom. She held it with both hands, not to steady it, but to steady herself. The world appeared to wobble and sway even though the broom sat grounded with its yellow bristles resting in the short grass. Tina tried to focus on the policeman, but the mustached officer kept slipping out of focus and turning into grim-faced twins.

"No, officer," Tina said. She paused to consider her words. She hadn't just slurred the word "officer" had she?

"You were flying erratically, and over a designated residential area." Fatherly disappointment tinged the policeman's rumbling baritone. "License and registration, please."

Tina looked down at the broom beneath her legs. She normally flew a vintage wooden-handled model with long, straw bristles. The lime green aluminum shaft beneath her looked alien in her hands. The saddle bags where she stowed her wand and registration were nowhere to be seen.

"Uhm ..." Tina said.

"Is there a problem?"

Tina looked back up at the policeman. She might have found him attractive in another setting, with his broad shoulders, dark hair, and well-trimmed mustache. At that moment, with his eyes narrowed and his arms crossed across his chest, she didn't find him attractive at all.

"This isn't my broom," Tina said.

Tina looked down at herself. Her cherry red dress still looked cute, though there were dark smudges at her hips and across her thighs. She couldn't remember how she'd dirtied her dress, but in her present tipsy haze, she hoped she'd had fun, whatever it was she'd been doing. She had a small purse slung over her shoulder that matched her dress. The tip of her wand stuck out the top of the small handbag. She reached for her purse, hoping she'd at least be able to provide her driver's license.

"Whoa, easy!" The policeman's hand hovered over the police issue rod slung at his hip as he stared at Tina's wand.

Tina let go of the broom to raise both hands. Her impaired balance failed her and she slipped from her broom. Arms windmilling, a rush of air pulling her hair back, she cried out in surprise. The policeman didn't have a chance to move. Tina fell into him. His footing slipped in the damp grass. They both crashed to the ground. The policeman grunted as Tina's weight landed on his belly.

"Sorry!" Tina said, her voice little more than a squeak.

The policeman pushed Tina off him with one rough swipe. He scrambled to his feet, his short, police-issue wand drawn and directed towards Tina.

"Don't move!" the policeman shouted.

Tina moved. She couldn't help herself. Seeing the weapon pointed at her, she let out another small cry and raised her hands. A blast echoed through the night. It sounded like a piano crashing onto concrete.

Lights flickered on in the windows of the closest houses, the neighborhood blinking awake with surprise. Tina flinched, her eyes pressed shut. She waited, expecting the curdling black fingers of a doom curse, or the searing heat of a flame shock.

She waited. Nothing happened. The echo of the mysterious spell faded beneath the sounds of a cricket's serenade, and the howl of a distant hound.

"Jeeze, Tina," a woman said.

Tina opened one eye, then the other. Her best friend Alexa stood over her, a mischievous smile twisting her lips. With one hand on her hip and the other holding her wand, Alexa looked like a burglar dressed head to toe in black.

Moonlight gathered around Alexa's head in a silver halo. Standing there with her breath forming steam in the cool night air, Alexa could have been an avenging angel swooping in to save her. But Tina knew her friend. Alexa was less a divine bringer of justice and more a devilish imp.

Alexa slid her wand into a pocket and reached down. Tina grasped the offered hand and allowed Alexa to haul her to her unsteady feet.

"Jeeze, Tina," Alexa repeated. "I can't believe this happened again."

"What do you mean 'again'?"

"Never mind. Come on. Get yourself together. I need your help."

Tina brushed the front of her dress. She failed to wipe away the new dark smudges she'd acquired from falling on the ground. Bending forward, with her balance still impaired, she started to fall again. Alexa caught her and held her up.

"This won't do," Alexa said.

"Shhhhh!" Tina tried to cover Alexa's lips with one finger, but Alexa batted her hand away.

"I didn't think you had that much to drink."

"I didn't. I had just enough."

Still holding Tina up with one hand, Alexa reached into another pocket and drew out a small vial.

"No, no," Tina said. "Shh. I've had enough."

"Stop shushing me and drink this. It will help."

Tina tried to take the vial, but her hands kept passing through empty air. She wobbled, and Alexa had to catch her again to keep her from falling.

"Okay, okay," Alexa said. "Just hold still. Here."

Alexa twisted around and under Tina, pulling one of Tina's arms across her shoulders. With her free hand, Alexa brought the vial to her mouth and took the cork stopper between her teeth. The stopper came free with a quiet pop. Alexa reached up with the arm supporting Tina's back, taking hold of Tina's dark blond hair. With an impish smile twisting her lips, Alexa gave Tina's hair a savage pull. Tina opened her mouth to protest, and Alexa poured in the vial.

The potion had a strange sweet and floral taste, like lilacs and honey. The fluid rushed to the back of Tina's throat, and she could either swallow or choke. Tina gulped loudly and a warm, tingling sensation radiated out from her belly into her extremities, rising up and warming her cheeks. She looked at her friend, still holding Tina up with one hand on her back.

Tina still saw double, but the tingling sensation began to settle behind her eyes. The twin images of Alexa slid together to form a single, smiling face. Tina's thoughts cleared. The half-giddy tipsiness evaporated, leaving her feeling warm but empty.

"What was that?" Tina asked.

"A little something I picked up from Mother Nature."

"Oh? How is she these days?"

"She has her hands full."

With her mind cleared, Tina pulled loose from Alexa and looked around. The broom she'd been riding still rested in the air a few feet away, the nose pointed up at a forty-five-degree angle. Several of the houses still had lights on in the windows, but no one appeared to be coming out to investigate the commotion.

"Where is the officer that pulled me over?"

Alexa looked around. "I don't see anyone here. It's probably not that important right now."

"Not important? What on Earth did you do?" Tina knelt and examined the ground. If Alexa had turned the cop into a caterpillar or something, they were both going to be in serious trouble.

"Relax," Alexa said. "Wherever he is, I'm sure he's fine. Come on. Get up before you make your dress even dirtier."

Tina rose back to her feet and looked at her dress again. She tried wiping away a particularly dark smudge at her hip. Her fussing did nothing but spread the dark spot over a wider area.

"All the magic in the world won't be able to get these stains out," Tina said.

"Forget about the dress for a moment. This is important. I'll get you a new one if you help me out."

Tina tilted her head as she studied her friend. She couldn't remember the last time she'd seen Alexa so serious or concerned.

"What's wrong?"

"I'll explain it on the way to my place." Alexa turned towards the green-handled vehicle and frowned. "Is that going to be able to carry us both? It looks like a small step up from a Swiffer."

Tina extended her hand and the broom responded. It snapped up and flew into Tina's grasp, as quick and sturdy as any broom she'd flown. "It feels solid enough. We'll fly low, just in case."

•　　•　　•

With the cool winter air whipping past them, Tina had trouble hearing Alexa's words. Her friend clung to her back and leaned forward to put the words directly in Tina's ears, but Tina could only catch every other one.

After a few minutes' flight, Tina tilted the broom down and settled it in a soft landing on Alexa's balcony. Alexa's cat, Barney, scooted out of the way of the landing broom. In a tabby colored blur, it ducked through the kitty door and into the apartment.

"You're going to have to repeat all of that," Tina said. She stepped off the broom and extended a hand to Alexa.

"What, all of it?" Alexa accepted Tina's help off the broom and stretched her legs.

"All I heard was something about your work getting out of hand."

Alexa drew a set of keys from one of her pockets and slipped one into the lock on the door. With a click and a squeak, the door opened. Alexa gestured with one hand, inviting Tina into her home, past the threshold.

Just inside, Tina turned to her friend. "You wouldn't happen to have some seltzer water or something, would you? Maybe I can still save my dress."

"There's some in the fridge." Alexa gestured towards the tiny kitchen on the other side of the apartment. "It might be a little flat. I opened it the other night before I realized I was out of gin. When you're ready, I'll tell you what happened. Again."

Though the apartment was small, Tina liked what Alexa had done with it. Family photos and oil paintings decorated the walls amongst the various wards and sigils worked into the wallpaper. Candles and lamps flared into life as soon as Tina stepped into the living room, the light sources providing ample, warm illumination. The light banished shadows both real and supernatural without feeling harsh or overpowering. Comfortable, second-hand furniture filled the small living space. Tina selected a chair with large, puffy cushions and sat down.

Alexa sat on the couch. She leaned forward, resting her elbows on her knees. She took a deep breath before launching into another explanation.

"You know what I do for a living, right?"

"Sure." Tina poured some of the seltzer onto a washcloth and scrubbed at the worst damage on her dress. "You're a clerk at Government House."

"No. Well, sort of. I'm one of the local liaisons between the state government and supernatural entities."

"Right. Government clerk."

Alexa sighed, then pressed on. "Anyways. New Years is coming, so a delegation was sent to prepare for the celebrations and rituals. Mother Nature, Father Time, and Baby New Year."

"Baby New Year?" Tina asked. "I thought Baby New Year wasn't born until after the first."

Alexa shrugged. "These are beings that exist outside the normal order. The way you and I think of time doesn't really apply to them. Especially not Baby New Year."

"Okay, fine. So what did you do? You didn't do something to the baby, did you?"

"Oh no. Baby New Year's fine. Mother Nature is taking care of him. The problem is Father Time."

Tina stopped scrubbing long enough to cover her eyes with one hand. "I must have heard some of this on the broom. I'm feeling a weird deja vu."

"First of all, what happened with Father Time was not my fault. When you look at Father Time, you see an old man. His hair is white, his hands shake, and he walks slow. So, when he asked if I'd help him to the roof so that he could look at the Moon, I said sure. No problem. I held his hand as we climbed the stairs. I opened the door for him and helped him step outside. Then he laughed and just disappeared."

"You lost Father Time?"

"I didn't lose him. He ran away."

Tina sat back in her chair. "Well, I don't see what the big deal is. Either he'll come back on his own or the city will have to do the rituals without him."

"I don't think you understand. We need him. Some of the most important rites won't work without him. If he's not present, a whole lot of spells the city depends on will start to break down. And we won't be able to fix it for a whole year."

"Can we get someone to fill in for him? Santa Claus is strong with time magic."

Alexa shook her head. "He's too busy this time of year. I tried getting through to his office the other day on a separate matter and it was just impossible. If they were smart, they'd start doing that 'Christmas in July' thing so they wouldn't be so jammed up in December."

"I think we're getting off topic. If Father Time teleported off the roof, you're never going to find him. He's an Old One. He could be anywhere in the world."

Alexa grew quiet. She clasped her hands in front of her and smiled her most mischievous smile. A smile that Tina had seen several times, always right before they both wound up in trouble.

"Uh oh," Tina said.

"He teleported, but I have three of his hairs." Alexa reached into a pocket and drew out a plain white envelope. "I might not be able to find Father Time with this, but I bet you can."

"Oh no." Tina held up her hands as if warding off an attack. "I'm not supposed to use tracking spells without a judge's approval. It's the law."

"This is important, Tina. Terrible things will happen if we don't get Father Time back for the rituals. Clocks will stop working. Trains will stop arriving when they're supposed to. Some spells won't work at all anymore. Do you know how many city functions rely on a proper yearly time ritual? Lots."

"But Father Time is an Old One. Do you know how much Old Ones hate being tracked?"

Alexa waved the argument away. "If Father Time didn't want to be found, he wouldn't have left the hair behind. He's an Old One, like you said."

Tina shook her head. "There's got to be another way. Have you talked to Mother Nature? Surely she can do something to bring him back."

"I did talk to her. She said that he does this sometimes, and then she gave me that potion you took earlier."

Tina stood up and began pacing. The living room was small, but Tina used what space she had while occasionally scrubbing at the stubborn stains on her dress. "I don't know, Alexa. I just don't know."

"If you don't help me, I could lose my job. Whether he tricked me or not, Father Time was my responsibility. Come on, don't make me beg."

Tina stopped pacing. She closed her eyes, hung her head, and sighed. "Okay. Fine. I'll help you. But when this is all said and done, you're going to owe me big time."

•   •   •

The night air rushed past Tina and Alexa as the green-handled broom soared above the city streets. A glowing ball floated just in front of the broom, dipping and weaving at random intervals, leading the witches in a generally eastern direction. One of Father Time's hairs burned within the ball of light, giving Tina's tracking spell the energy and guidance it needed to do its job. City lights blurred beneath them as they soared onward, houses and buildings appearing and disappearing as shadowy, indistinct shapes below.

The tracking spell slowed and dropped towards the earth. The broom followed the spell's descent. Tina recognized the downtown area, the streets illuminated by tall lamps and neon signs. Christmas decorations sparkled like captured starlight, giving the city a surreal, heavenly glow. When the tracking spell came to a halt, Tina and Alexa lowered their feet to the pavement in front of a high-class restaurant: Claire De Lune's.

"He's in there," Tina said. "I'll wait out here."

"Ha ha. Yeah, right." Alexa let go of Tina and climbed off the broom. "You're not getting out of this that easy."

"You needed me to cast the tracking spell. I did it, and I flew you here."

"But I still need your help. He gave me the slip once already."

Tina sighed. She pulled up on the broom and guided it to a proper parking space. She grounded it, the plastic bristles brushing dust clear from a small patch of concrete. Tina reached for where the saddle bags should have been before remembering that they weren't there. This was not her broom. Then she looked at the next parking space over.

"How did you get here?" Tina took a few steps towards the familiar vehicle. She laid a hand on the hard wood, then opened the bag hanging from the closest side. Inside, she saw a registration card with her name printed across the top.

"Huh," Alexa said, stepping up next to Tina.

"Did you know this was here?"

Alexa shook her head. "When Father Time took off, he didn't use a broom. He just disappeared."

Tina put a hand on her broom, hoping that the touch would jog her memory. She couldn't remember anything from that night before taking Mother Nature's potion. She thought she'd been celebrating, but she couldn't remember why.

"I guess it doesn't matter," Tina said. She gestured, and the tracking spell with its still burning hair separated from the green broom and floated towards the restaurant door. "Let's just get this over with."

A crowd of people hovered near the door with their hands in their pockets and their jackets pulled tight. Their breath puffed into steam as they waited for their names to be called. Tina and Alexa stepped past them, following the glowing orb.

More people stood just inside the door and the heat of the place pressed down on Tina like a hen smothering her chicks. She slowed down a step. The tracking spell flickered before Tina regained her composure and concentration. While refocusing the spell, she accidentally bumped into an older woman in the ugliest Christmas sweater she'd ever seen.

The woman turned towards Tina, her lips peeling back from her teeth as she sucked in a sharp breath. For a moment, Tina thought the woman was about to curse her. Before the ugly-sweatered woman could launch an attack, Alexa stepped in and spoke quiet words to her. Whatever Alexa said seemed to work. The strange woman turned away, revealing the back of the sweater, just as hideous as it appeared on the front.

"How many?" The maître d's haughty tone pulled Tina's attention away from the sweater.

"Oh. The person we're meeting is already here."

"What's the name for your party?"

"We won't be staying to eat. We're just looking for someone."

"I'm sorry, but you'll have to-"

Tina cut the host off with two quick motions. She pulled her badge from her re-acquired bag and thrust it a few inches from the maître d's face. "We're going to walk around and find the person we're looking for. Understand?"

The maître d' took a step back, raising his hands in a defensive gesture. Tina nodded and stepped forward, following the remains of her tracking spell into the dining area.

"You went for the badge," Alexa said, stepping up to walk beside Tina. "You never go for the badge."

"We don't have a lot of time." Tina gestured towards the ball of light. "The hair is almost spent."

"We have two more."

"Yeah, but we don't want to use them if we don't have to. It's better to ..."

Tina's words faded. She looked past the spell and saw a man sitting at a table by himself. Tall even while sitting down, the man had black hair with a shock of white running down the center like a skunk's stripe. He wore an immaculate black suit with a white silk tie. He looked like a man in his mid-forties, lean, with strong cheek bones and trimmed gray goatee covering his chin.

"That's him," Alexa whispered. "He looks different than when he left the capitol, but that's definitely him."

"What's the plan?" Tina kept her own voice down to a whisper.

Before Alexa could respond, Father Time looked up. His silver-blue eyes focused on the ball of light hovering halfway between his table and Tina. He reached up with one hand, snapped his fingers, and the spell burst like a popped balloon.

"Get him!" Alexa shouted.

Tina stumbled forward. Alexa pushed past her. Alexa clapped a hand around Father Time's wrist.

"Gotcha!" Alexa said.

Father Time looked down at Alexa's hand. He raised his eyes to her face. A wicked smile spread across his lips. And then he disappeared with a boom like thunder as the air rushed into the space where he had been.

"Gotcha?" Tina asked. "That was your plan?"

Alexa opened her mouth to respond. Before she could form words, the table beneath her cracked. She jumped away, pulling her hand to her chest. The table began to crumble where the wood cracked, dust and ash falling and drifting away with the stirring of the air.

"Alexa, what did you do?"

"I didn't do anything!"

Tina pointed her wand at the still disintegrating table and cast a divination spell. Symbols made from raw magic formed in the air above the table, listing out properties of the magic in an arcane script.

"What is it?" Alexa asked.

"Time," Tina said. "There is a bubble moving forward in time very quickly. The table is falling apart due to old age."

Alexa held up the hand she'd used to grab Father Time. She frowned and wiggled her fingers.

"It looks like you were protected," Tina said. "He didn't want to hurt anyone."

"So this is a warning."

"Looks that way."

Alexa reached into a pocket and pulled out the white envelope. "Well, we still have a couple strands of hair left."

Tina closed her eyes, lowered her head, and covered her face with her palm. It looked like it was going to be a long night.

•   •   •

Another hair burned within the confines of a tracking spell, and Tina's sturdy wooden broom followed the ball of light and magic through the night air. Alexa clung to Tina's back. Tina guided the broom in its flight, the city streaking by below.

After a while, the buildings became shorter, thinning out until the witches flew over the tops of trees and open countryside. The city lights no longer spread out below them but glinted from behind. A highway stretched its long arm from the cluster of lights and buildings behind them, reaching across undeveloped land towards an oasis in the desert. A small cluster of neon that Tina knew to be a casino.

Tina settled the broom just outside the casino grounds. She stepped off and looked up at the sign.

"Tazon de la Luna," Alexa said.

"First a restaurant, now a casino," Tina said. "Don't you liaisons entertain the guests?"

"We give them whatever they want, within reason."

"So why is Father Time doing this?"

"You can ask him after we catch him."

Tina led Alexa across the parking area and through the main entrance of the casino. The sounds of bells ringing and coins collecting in trays rang out through the room, the percussive music of money changing hands. A cheer rose from a craps table nearby. The continuous murmur of conversations floated across the room like foam floating atop a churning sea.

A few steps past the threshold, and the tracking spell flickered and died. The charred remains of the hair powering the spell floated to the carpet in front of Tina.

"Huh." Tina bent down and picked up the hair. Probably not enough to make a spell out of, but it didn't seem wise to just leave it where anyone could pick it up. "Anti-magic field in the casino. That makes sense."

"That upsets my plan a bit," Alexa said.

"Oh? You mean, you came up with something more than yelling 'Get him'?"

Alexa elbowed Tina in the ribs. "I was thinking we'd trap him in a circle. We could use some of the hair to make it binding."

Tina looked around the casino. On the walls, pillars, and ceiling, she could see the etched runes holding the anti-magic field in place. While many people had wands visibly on their person, no one was casting any spells. And yet, throughout the room, Tina could see evidence of magic at work.

A fountain floated several feet off the floor, its sapphire water leaping from shafts and dancing in the air before splashing back into the basin. Several brooms wandered through the room, dipping and swaying like dancers, sweeping the carpets clean.

"Magic objects work here," Tina said. "If a spell is bound to an object, it keeps working, but new spells are blocked."

"We can work with that. We'll put a circle on a blanket or sheet. Then when we find him, we throw it on him, and he won't be able to get away."

Tina frowned but said nothing.

"Why don't you make the circle trap," Alexa said. "I'll go through the casino until I find Father Time. We can meet back here."

Tina drew in a deep breath and exhaled through her nose. "Okay. Try not to spook him."

With another flash of her badge, Tina acquired suitable material with the help of one of the casino staff. The custodian produced a sheet from the hotel, a permanent marker, and one of the restaurant's saltshakers. Tina thanked the staff member, then took the material out to the parking lot.

Like the tracker spell, the binding circle fell into a category of magic that Tina employed regularly for her job.

After a quick mental checklist, she laid the sheet out on the ground and drew a circle as large and as perfect as she could. The circle didn't have to be perfect, of course. It just needed to be closed. Tina preferred her spells to look neat and tidy. A nice, round circle looked better than a sloppy oval. Once she satisfied herself with the shape of the enchantment, Tina poured the salt evenly around the inside. If she had more, she could have made the entire circle with the salt. That was the proper recipe, after all. But lining the inside of a closed circle would suffice, and that's all she could do with what she had at hand.

She placed the final ingredient, the charred fragment of hair from the tracker spell, onto the circle so that it touched both the ink and the salt. The hair was too small to power a spell on its own, but it would do for providing a sympathetic connection between the subject and the trap. With all the ingredients in place, Tina drew her wand, said the words to give the spell power, and released it.

Thin gray smoke rose from the sheet. Tina leaned down and examined the circle. She could see where the spell wove into the fabric, looping faint lines of power around the ink and salt, binding the ingredients into a single, magical object. As long as the circle remained closed, the subject wouldn't be able to leave. All they had to do now was put the subject in the trap.

Tina folded the sheet into a neat square, then returned to the entrance hall of the casino. She found Alexa waiting for her.

"It's done?" Alexa asked.

Tina held up the folded sheet and nodded.

"Perfect. I found him at one of the poker tables. I don't think he saw me."

"Before we go, what's the actual plan this time?"

"I'll go around and come at him from the front. When he sees me, you throw the sheet over him. Then we'll guide him out and take him back to the capitol."

Tina looked down at the sheet. She considered the plan for several moments before responding. "This isn't much better than what we tried at the restaurant."

"Sure it is. The spell is all prepared. What could go wrong?"

Alexa led the way. They walked around blackjack tables and rows and rows of slot machines. Chips exchanged hands or dropped into one-armed bandits all around Tina and Alexa. The thick crowds of desperate gamblers around the room made it difficult for them to get through. After a few minutes of side-stepping and muttered apologies, they reached the poker tables. Alexa held up her hand, then slipped off to her right. Tina watched her go before turning her attention to the tables.

Father Time sat with his back to her. He looked as he had in the restaurant, with his black suit and short, white-striped hair. Tina could see an impressive stack of chips in front of The Old One. One of Father Time's neighbors said something Tina couldn't quite make out, and all the players erupted in laughter, including Father Time. He picked up a short glass, raised it to the speaker, and took a sip.

Tina could see Alexa approaching Father Time's table from the other side. Tina started forward, unfolding some of the sheet and preparing for the throw. They would only get one shot at this. If she missed …

"You!" Father Time shouted.

Tina hurried forward. The sheet flew from her hands. Father Time started to get up from the table. The other players turned, their eyes going wide.

The Old One started to do something with one of his hands. Before he could work his magic, the sheet covered him. He tried to get free, but the spell held. Father Time lowered himself back to the chair, the sheet draped around him.

"Yes!" Alexa shouted.

"What's the meaning of this?" the dealer asked.

Other players started to raise their concerns. Tina stepped forward and raised her badge.

"This is city business," Tina said, using what she thought of as The Voice of Authority. It wasn't magic, but it often worked better than any spell in her book. "Dealer, please cash our friend out. Have his winnings sent to the capitol."

Alexa stepped up to one side of Father Time. Tina took the other. Holding him between them, the two witches pulled him to his feet and guided him through the casino. Players and casino workers alike gave the three strange looks, but Tina ignored it. Whatever disruption they'd caused died as quickly as it was born as the gamblers turned back to their games.

"It's a good, strong spell," Father Time said.

"Thank you," Tina said.

"It's almost perfect."

"Almost?" Alexa asked.

"I can't step out or cast my will beyond the circle, but there's nothing stopping me from applying it inside."

"We're in an anti-magic zone," Tina said.

"Are we?" Father Time asked.

The sheet began to disintegrate from within, the individual threads yellowing before crumbling to dust. Tina and Alexa stopped in their tracks. Before they could do anything, the hole in the sheet expanded, entropy accelerating along the fabric. The hole reached the edge of the circle, broke it, and with another pop and rush of air, Father Time disappeared.

"Damn it!" Alexa said.

"What the hell?" someone yelled from one of the slot machines.

"What are you trying to pull?" A player shouted at a dealer at one of the blackjack tables.

More shouts and complaints arose. People stood from their stools. Gamblers shook angry fists at dealers. All around Tina and Alexa, the casino began to erupt in anger and unpowered curses.

Tina looked around. Some slot machines were frozen, their dials caught in mid-spin. Others appeared to be spinning constantly. At a nearby craps table, Tina could see the dice tumbling and tumbling, showing no sign of stopping. Cards were frozen in place. Roulette wheels refused to slow down to drop the ball in a slot. Throughout the casino, it looked like all the rules of causality had been broken. No winners. No losers. Just a whole bunch of frustrated gamblers.

"We need to get out of here," Tina said.

"No argument here," Alexa said.

They left.

• • •

Tina and Alexa stood outside the casino next to Tina's wooden broom. The warmth spells worked into the fabric of Tina's dress were barely holding back the bite of the frigid winter air.

"One last hair," Alexa said.

Tina took the envelope from Alexa, fished out the hair, and held it between thumb and forefinger. "This is our last chance. We better make it count."

Once again, Tina cast the tracking spell. The ball of light rose into the air. Tina and Alexa followed on the broom. They leaned into the wind and turned towards the city, the tracking spell streaking ahead of them like a shooting star.

The tracking spell took them back to the city, but only to the edge. When Tina parked her broom, she landed in front of a small bar that didn't appear to have an obvious name. Neon signs in the windows declared the popular brands of alcohol the bar offered on tap. Most of the signs flickered or appeared completely broken. The only sign in full working condition said "Blue Moon".

"I'm seeing a pattern," Tina said.

"Oh?"

"Come on. Let me do the planning this time."

Tina led the way into the bar with Alexa right behind. The dim interior smelled like spilled beer and stale cigar smoke. A young couple dressed in leather and denim played pool in one corner. Another pair of gruff, bearded men threw darts at a board. Most of the tables sat empty. At the bar, a skinny brunette in a shirt too skimpy for the winter weather served drinks to the only person sitting on a stool. Father Time.

"Just wait here," Tina said.

"But--"

"Wait here!"

Alexa wilted. Tina patted her shoulder before turning and walking the half dozen steps to the bar. She started to pull out a stool, then stopped.

"Mind if I join you?" she asked.

"Please!" Father Time said.

Tina sat down. She saw the tall glass of amber liquid in front of The Old One. An orange slice hung off the lip. She gestured to the glass and spoke to the bartender. "I'll have what he's having."

"Put it on my tab," Father Time said.

The bartender produced a clean glass, filled it from one of the taps, slotted an orange slice onto it, and set it in front of Tina. Tina raised it to Father Time. Father Time mirrored the gesture with his own glass. They took a sip together.

"Is your friend not joining us?" Father Time asked.

"She might. I thought it would be better if you and I talked first."

Out of the corner of her eye, Tina saw one of the dart players stumble after a toss. He caught himself on the edge of the bar, but not before spilling an entire bowl of peanuts. The waitress looked up, fire in her eyes.

"Jimmy, you're cut off!" she shouted.

Jimmy responded by showing the waitress his middle finger.

"What's on your mind?" Father Time asked.

"That's what I was going to ask you," Tina said. "You told Alexa that you wanted to see the moon, and you've gone all over the place. A restaurant. A casino. And now this bar. What are you looking for?"

"I didn't lie to dear Alexa. In fact, I am incapable of lying. The restaurant, Claire De Lune's. It means moonlight. Tazon de la Luna is the bowl of the moon. And now I'm drinking this. I wanted to see the moon, and now I've seen its reflection in three places."

"But why? What's so special about the moon tonight?"

Father Time laughed. "What's so special about the moon any night? Her face is always changing, and yet, it's always the same. She waxes and she wanes. She pulls and pushes the tides. Constant and shifting. Always moving, but always steady. And she's old. Like me."

Tina paused to collect her thoughts. She watched the waitress leave the bar, ducking into a back room.

"This isn't about the moon," Tina said. "It's about you, isn't it?"

"Soon, I'm going to face my death," Father Time said. "Just as I faced it last year. Just as I will face it again next year. Always the same, but constantly changing. A continuous cycle. Like the shifting face of the moon."

Motion from the door caught Tina's attention. She turned to see Alexa hopping up and down. With a reluctant nod, Tina invited Alexa to join them.

Alexa took the stool on the other side of Father Time. "What's going on?"

"Your friend and I were just catching up," Father Time said. "Do you intend on trying to apprehend me again? I can assure you that it will not work."

"I just need to make sure you're there for the ceremony," Alexa said.

"I said I would be there. And I cannot lie. I will be there."

"But —"

"It's okay," Tina said. "Alexa, you should go. I'll stay with Father Time until he's ready to return. You should probably take a cab, anyway. All three of us won't fit on my broom."

Alexa drew in a deep breath and let it out in a sigh. "Are you sure?"

"It'll be fine," Tina said. "I'll catch up with you later."

Alexa slipped off her stool, stepped around Father Time, and gave Tina a hug. "Thank you. Be careful."

"I will," Tina said.

Alexa turned and left, pulling a cell phone from her pocket as she slipped out the door.

"She's a good girl, but she tries too hard," Father Time said. "When she dotes on us like she does, it makes us feel our age. Which, as you know, is considerable."

"You were saying something about facing your death."

"You try too hard, too." Father Time smiled before taking a long sip from his glass.

The waitress returned to the bar with a broom and a dustpan. She went to where Jimmy had spilled the peanuts, bent down, and began sweeping up the mess.

"You can't understand what it's like living the same moments, over and over, with no hope of changing the future," Father Time said. "You humans are blessed with short lives. They're fast and interesting, full of love and laughter and pain and sorrow. They move, like stones cast in a lake, skipping along and creating ripples across time."

"I'm trying to understand," Tina said.

Father Time cast a glance towards the waitress. He turned back to Tina with a smile. "Yes. I think you are trying to understand. Maybe I'll help you with that. But to answer your question, I decided to take the night off. Have a nice meal. Play some cards. Have a drink. Is that so wrong?"

Tina shook her head. "No. That sounds like a nice way to spend an evening."

The waitress finished cleaning up the mess, propped the broom by the door, and stepped outside to dump the dustpan. Tina studied the broom for a moment, sipping her beer. It looked familiar, but she couldn't quite place where she'd seen it before.

Father Time and Tina made small talk. By the time Tina had finished her glass, the couple at the pool table had left, and the gruff dart players were sitting at a table. Tina felt the effects of the alcohol hitting her harder than she expected. Served her right for drinking on an empty stomach.

"I should go," Tina said. "I feel like I've been up all night."

"No," Father Time said. "The night is still young. How about just one more, for the road? This will be the last time around, I promise."

Tina looked at the broom still leaning next to the door. It had a green metal handle and short yellow bristles. It had been made for sweeping, but Tina thought she could make it fly.

"One more, for the road," Tina said. "Why not?"

About the Authors

As one of seven children, it's little wonder that Melissa Buhl's first story concerns itself with witches and witchcraft. Melissa is a voracious reader. When her nose isn't in a book, she works as a sales assistant in the health insurance industry. Melissa quilts, and has been known to play clarinet from time to time. With her husband, Brian, she has raised two beautiful and intelligent children, Bryanna and Christopher.

Hailing from sunny Sacramento, California, Brian Buhl is trying to save the world. Formerly enlisted in the U.S. Air Force, Brian now spends most of his time writing software for the solar industry. When he's not engineering technical solutions, he can sometimes be found playing saxophone with local community bands. Also, he writes science fiction and fantasy.

Also By The Author

THE REPOSSESSED GHOST
by Brian C. E. Buhl

Do you think ghosts haunt only houses?

As a repo man, Mel just pulled off the smoothest take of his life. Kate, a college student, was undecided on which major to pursue. All of their plans went out the window the night Mel found Kate in the back of a '74 Nova.

Available in hardcover, trade paperback, and digital editions from
Water Dragon Publishing
waterdragonpublishing.com